In My MAGiCAL BUBBLE

WRITTEN BY PAOLA ANDREA FERNÁNDEZ DE SOTO ABDULRAHIN

ILLUSTRATED BY LUZ ADRIANA MAÑOZCA

JAKOB KAMIL GUZIAK is the inspiration behind this magical children´s book. He is an ADA SCID toddler, also known as a "Bubble Boy." Jakob was born in August 2019 with no immune system to fight infections or colds. Every day he must fight to survive his condition and medical expectations. He loves to dance and watch the birds, and through his story, Jakob hopes to raise awareness about ADA SCID; gene therapy; blood, plasma, and stem cell donation.

Visit his Twitter, Instagram, or Facebook blog @jakoblittlefighter.

To your soul for choosing me in this life.
Promise to look for me in the next one.

FriesenPress

One Printers Way
Altona, MB, ROG OBO
Canada

www.friesenpress.com

Illustrated by Luz Adriana Mañozca

ISBN
978-1-03-912403-5 (Hardcover)
978-1-03-912402-8 (Paperback)
978-1-03-912404-2 (eBook)

1. JUVENILE FICTION, BIOGRAPHICAL

Distributed to the trade by The Ingram Book Company

In my MAGICAL BUBBLE

Written by Paola Andrea Fernández de Soto AbdulRahin
Illustrated by Luz Adriana Mañozca

Magic is when we wake up on Friday,
and it's the International Day of Dirtiness.

I am Super Jakob, and my loyal best buddy Buvo
and I are off to puddle land on a rainbow unicorn.

In my morning jungle, Buvo and I love to jump
and swing from trees while the monkeys sing
fruit songs in our ears.

"Breakfast is ready!" yells Mom.
"Wash your hands and the magic horse."
"Argh, come on!" I say.

SHHH...

Mommy calls it the phone,
but I know it is a super-powerful
teleporter and magnifying glass.

Grammy sends her muffins through it
and Grandpa sends his love.
Buvo likes to pop Grandpa's hearts
over the fruit and watch them
turn into colourful, tasty sprinkles.
My favourite flavour is choco-majestic,
but Mom says that choco-majestic
requires majestic cleaning.

Did I mention that I am
a marvelous painter?

Buvo likes to
call himself: **THE GENIE OF
THE CANVAS.**

He says **OLÉ!** here
and
"OLÉ"
there

and sings a CHA CHA CHA song.
LOOK AT OUR MUSEUM WALL!

"Soap, soap, soap time," says Mom.

Lunch time is under-the-sea time. Today there was a

SHARK ATTACK

HURRY.

Are you ready for a secret? If the afternoon gets boring, the best cure of all is to share a lollipop with a friend.

But **SHHH!** Buvo always brings his mango germilicious one.

And then we say,

GIVE ME AN S,
GIVE ME AN O,
GIVE ME AN A,
GIVE ME A P!

"Team Soap, let's go!"
cheers Dad.

Daddy often says that **FIGHTER** is my middle name. **TADAA!** With my armor on and my sword high in the sky, I'm ready to fight danger, dragons, and fire.

"Uh oh, Your Majesty. What is going on?" asks Dad.

OH NO. I FEEL SICK. AM I SICK?

This is not good. "Buvo, get the sick list please,"
I say a rash, a bump?
No, wait a minute—it might be a cold. I feel green,
I feel dizzy, I think it was the lollipop.

"SOMEBODY CALL THE FIREFIGHTERS!

I feel like I am going to explode."

"Jakob, it's okay to be afraid. Everything
will be fine," says Dad.
"Put your sword down; it's time to go."

Whenever things get out of control, I know it's time for extra courage, extra muscle, and tons of love. Dr. Mustache will fix me in no time.

"Don't be sad, Buvo. Please wait for me. The day is not done."

"The bubble-mobile is ready. Let's go," says Dad.

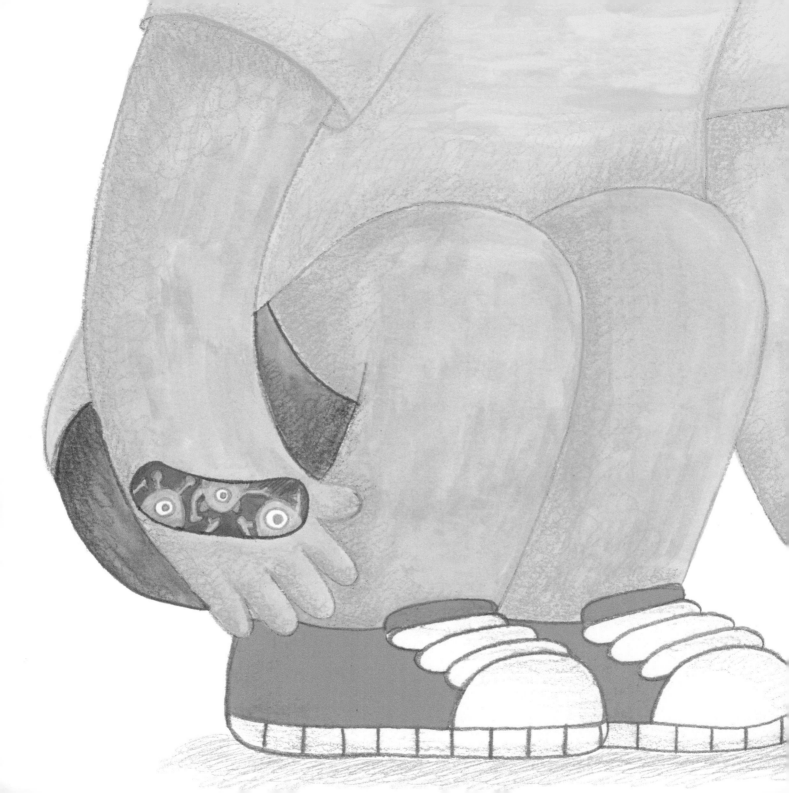

On my return to the magical bubble,

I FEEL LIKE A GIANT.

I can reach the ceiling
with my wiggly toes.

I AM UNTOUCHABLE!.

"Buvo, I'm okay now. Don't be scared."

"Time for a bubble
bath!" says Mom.

With Mr. Buvo as our commander-in-chief,
Duck the Pirate and I navigate the dangerous
waters of the black sea.

With a **SPLASH** here

and a **SPLASH** there,

clean real good until
you say

HURRAY!

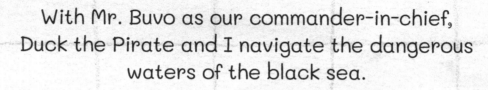

"Clean with a POP, POP, POP," says Mom.

It's time for bed, and I can touch the stars.
I think I am going to camp on the moon
tonight. I'll dream about the park, new
friends, and castles made of mud.

"Sweet dreams, our bubble boy,"
says Mom and Dad.

Debut author **PAOLA ANDREA FERNÁNDEZ DE SOTO ABDULRAHIN** is a screening officer by day and a blogger by night. She received her Bachelor of Arts in Advertising and Communication from Autónoma de Occidente University. In addition to working on her son´s blog and being a dedicated mother, she is also fighting her personal battle with cancer. Born in Colombia, and now living in Canada, Paola is a lover of naps, music, and all types of projects.

LUZ ADRIANA MAÑOZCA is a designer and illustrator for brands, packaging, web, and editorial projects. She finds inspiration on the streets of New York City, her new home. Ever since she was little, Luz's father read and illustrated children's books in their family home, which generated Luz's special interest in drawing. She studied graphic design and illustration for children's literature in Colombia, where she was born and raised. For more of Luz's work, visit www.lamodraws.com and follow her on social media @lamodraws.

DRAW YOUR FIGHTER POSE ON THE MUSEUM WALL.

You can colour on us.

Remember to clean your hands real good after!

MUSEUM WALL

Take a picture and tag me on instagram: @jakoblittlefighter

Lightning Source UK Ltd.
Milton Keynes UK
UKHW052228240522
403459UK00005B/293